P9-AOH-768

3 4028 08593 1294
HARRIS COUNTY PUBLIC LIBRARY

J Ghouls
Ghoulstone, Rotterly
Undead Ed and the fingers
    of doom

          $10.99
    ocn861068938
     01/19/2015

WITHDRAWN

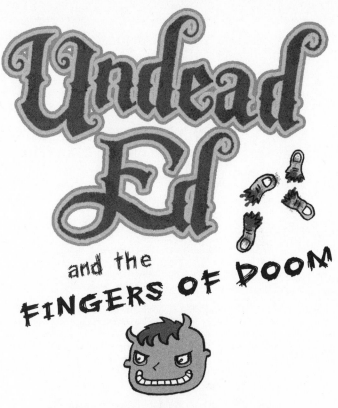

Undead Ed

and the
FINGERS OF DOOM

Rotterly Ghoulstone

ILLUSTRATED BY

Nigel Baines

An Imprint of Penguin Group (USA)

A division of Penguin Young Readers Group
Published by the Penguin Group
Penguin Group (USA) LLC
345 Hudson Street
New York, New York 10014

USA / Canada / UK / Ireland / Australia / New Zealand / India / South Africa / China
Penguin.com
A Penguin Random House Company

Text copyright © 2014 Rotterly Ghoulstone
Illustrations copyright © 2014 Nigel Baines

Penguin supports copyright. Copyright fuels creativity, encourages diverse voices, promotes free speech, and creates a vibrant culture. Thank you for buying an authorized edition of this book and for complying with copyright laws by not reproducing, scanning, or distributing any part of it in any form without permission. You are supporting writers and allowing Penguin to continue to publish books for every reader.

ISBN: 978-1-59514-534-5

Printed in the United States of America

1 3 5 7 9 10 8 6 4 2

This is a work of fiction. Names, characters, places, and incidents either are the product of the author's imagination or are used fictitiously, and any resemblance to actual persons, living or dead, businesses, companies, events, or locales is entirely coincidental.

To my beautiful daughter,
Evangeline Lilly Rose Stone.

REASON ...TO HATE MONDAY:

IT SUCKS

My name is Ed Bagley—and I'm dead meat.
Literally. You could go outside right now, dig
through the trash can, and find fish corpses
that look better than me.

Next to you, Bagley, I feel fantastic!

You may think you're ugly or that you smell or that you're having a really bad hair day. Well, get over it.

I'm uglier.

I'm smellier.

And I'm having a bad hair life . . . except that I'm not actually alive any more.

Walking. Corpse.

That's right, I'm a zombie—an unearthly freak in a crazy, bad world of blood-sucking, flesh-eating critters from the underworld.

Only it's not a complete nightmare for everyone—oh, no. Vampires are drop-dead gorgeous (see what I did there?), werewolves are all emotion and fury, ghosts are stylish with beautiful singing voices, and ghouls don't care what they munch on as long as it smells better than their own feet.

But zombies are a different story.

Here's the download of my current problems in five points, so all of you can understand them:

1. I stink like your grandma's toe jam.
2. My fat keeps falling off in lumps.
3. I'm going to end up like the skeleton hanging in your science teacher's classroom.
4. All my friends hate me.
5. Did I mention I stink?

That about covers it. For those of you

who've followed my hideous, depressing story from the beginning, I don't need to tell you how much trouble I'm in right now. For the rest of you, here's the quickest recap in the history of books:

Born.

Lived.

Hit by a truck.

Died.

Woke up a zombie.

Hope that fills in some of the blanks for you. If not, I'm really sorry about that. No, wait . . . I'm over it.

I've got my own problems, and they're far worse than yours.

Let's go back to number four on that list: all my friends hate me.

They didn't before, but they do now. I used to have two of the best friends a walking corpse could hope for. Then I did something really, pants-wettingly crazy and lost them both forever.

I killed someone—someone they both loved and respected. Someone even I loved and respected.

His name was Evil Clive, and like me, he was a zombie—but he was probably the nicest, most caring dead guy I ever met.

Before I evicted him, that is.

Eviction: that's death for the undead. No one (not even the ghosts, the ghouls, and the phantoms) knows what happens when a soul is evicted from its undead shell. I'm not in any hurry to find out, myself. I've died once—I'd prefer not to die twice.

Of course, I didn't mean to evict Clive.

His murder was actually the work of my evil left arm.

Er . . . I told you about that, right?

OMG, I didn't. Right, here goes: hold on tight for the quick version.

I was normal.

Left arm was normal.

Left arm got possessed by the demonic spirit of Kambo Cheapteeth.

I died, came back as a zombie.

Left arm decided we were growing apart and went out on its own like a talented drummer in a really lame rock band.

However, it tried to kill me first.

A lot.

REASON...TO FEAR MY HAND:

IT'S THE
DEVIL'S WORK

Apparently, no one in the undead community knew when the cell was built or who it was built for. All anyone knew for sure was that it was there, and trust me, that knowledge alone was bad enough.

Of course, there have always been tunnels under Mortlake. There are tunnels under pretty much every town here: sewer tunnels, wartime tunnels, old train tunnels.

Mortlake has all three. Beneath the town, there are the air-raid runs and the sewers. Below the sewers, there is the abandoned subway. And—deeper still—there is something called the Well.

The Well is basically a giant vertical drop with stairs that snake down around the outside. At the bottom is a single long, dank tunnel that runs to a door so well fortified that it might as well be made of the rock that surrounds it.

And behind that door . . .

. . . was me.

I sat in the darkness, my face streaked wet with grime and the tracks of my tears, wondering if my life could actually get any worse.

Of course, I'd had the odd visitor. Max and Jemini, my former best friends, had both been down to see me at various times—but the conversation was always a bit awkward. If you want my honest opinion, I don't think either of them trusted me anymore, and who could blame them? I was surprised anyone bothered to come and see me at all.

CLUNK.

Speak of the devil.

CLUNK.

CLUNK.

CLUNK.

The irregular and nearly deafening sound of the bolts sliding back signaled either a visitor or lunch—and considering I didn't eat . . .

Sure enough, the door yawned open and in stalked Max Moon, the werewolf.

Typically, my oldest and best friend in the world of the undead didn't look me directly in the eye, choosing instead to focus on a point about three centimeters over my forehead. I couldn't tell if this was because my jawbone was now completely bare of the tattered flesh that covered the rest of my face, or because he just couldn't bring himself to really lock eyes with such a mindless, moronic loser.

"Hey, Ed," he muttered. "Er . . . I've brought you some news from town."

I looked up at him and sniffed a bit. "Good news or bad news?"

"It's more like—bad and worse. Sorry, but it's mostly grim."

Max smiled weakly, but there was no

humor in it. I guess he felt as awful about the whole situation as I did.

"There's a big movement of hard-line Clive supporters who want to kill you for what happened. They've got a lot of ghouls, werewolves, and vampires working for them, too. They're at war with the council over it, and the whole thing's turning really violent."

"Awesome," I muttered, looking down at the floor. "I guess it's no more than I deserve. Anything else?"

Max swallowed a few times, and I knew whatever was coming was going to be bad.

"Yeah, kinda. The under-council had a meeting, and they've decided to do this ancient test thing to find out whether your arm killed Clive or you did."

"Right." I sniffed miserably and shuffled back against the wall, wincing as some of my exposed backbone brushed the rock. "I've never passed a test in my life, Max."

The werewolf shrugged and folded his arms.

"Well, if you fail this test, they're going to banish you from Mortlake."

"And if I pass?"

"If you pass, they're going to do something much worse. . . ."

"Well that's just gr—What? Say that last bit again."

I dragged myself to my feet and tried to make such a disgusting face that Max had no choice but to make eye contact with me. "Are you sure you haven't gotten those two punishments mixed up?"

The werewolf looked at the floor and shook his head, just as Jemini sidled into view behind him.

"What's she doing here?" I asked, wishing my voice didn't sound so whiny in the gloom.

The great door slammed shut again, locked from the outside by one of the countless haters I'd gathered following my destruction of the town leader.

"It's like this, Ed," Jemini said, moving forward, her tearful eyes making me wish she wasn't looking at me directly. "Either you killed Clive or the devil killed Clive through you. If it's the first case, you're no longer welcome in town. But if it's the second, well, that's really, really bad . . . even by your standards. You'd just be too dangerous to—"

"Wait a minute!" I shouted, trying to ignore the fact that my evil left hand was already twitching like an angry snake. "Can't I fight this? I mean, him?"

Max gaped at me. "The devil? Are you nuts?"

I stepped forward and resisted the urge to grab hold of Max's fur with my good hand.

"Listen," I snapped. "I've been run over, ripped open, smashed through a wall, bitten, cursed, and killed. Right now, I'd fight the devil and his entire army for what's

been done to me. I'm frightened of nothing and no one. I just want all my friends
back—because I'd rather be rat food than
live in a place where people think I evicted
Clive on purpose."

I half stomped, half slid into the far corner
of the room and collapsed into a miserable,
defiant heap.

Jemini cleared her throat. "At least if you
let them do the test, everyone will know you
weren't in control. I really think we should tell
the council that—"

"Tell them to bring it on," I roared. "Whatever test they want, whenever they want. I
don't care."

As my tears welled up, I curled into a ball in
the corner of the room and hid my face in the
crook of my increasingly bare elbow. I didn't
look up again until the door had opened and

shut, and I was left alone in the darkness with my own despair.

REASON ... TO AVOID CHEESE:

IT'S MAD, BAD, AND DANGEROUS TO CHASE

The test finally happened at what I guessed was about midafternoon the following day.

The bolts on the great door slid back as usual, but then there was silence.

Complete silence.

Like someone who has just entered a room to find everyone staring at him with weird smirks on their faces, I moved very cautiously, expecting some horrible event to occur at any moment.

This is the test, I thought. *Expect brutality.*

I reached the door unharmed and put an ear to the door (which turned out to be a mistake when I pulled away and the ear actually stayed stuck on the metal). There was an incredible lack of noise from the hallway beyond.

Nothing.

Slowly, carefully, I grasped the single iron handle on the great portal—and pulled.

Crreeeeeaaaaak.

The door swung toward me as I took several steps back—and there it was: a cold, empty passage filled with dark, gloomy shadows and only the distant flicker of torchlight.

The walls were slimy and covered in moss, the ceiling was crawling with weird insects (including something that looked like three eyeballs joined to a toe), and the floor was . . . er . . .

I looked down at the floor and did a double take.

Then I shook my head.

I even blinked to make sure I wasn't imagining things.

Nope.

There on the floor of the passage was a thick wedge of cheese attached to some sort of metal wire.

"Is this a joke?" I called out, nudging the cheese with my shoe. It moved a bit but not much. "What's the test? To see if I try to eat it?"

There was no reply, and I looked down again.

The wire pulled tight, and the cheese shifted about four centimeters.

I didn't quite know what to do, so I called out again.

"This is ridiculous! What can this possibly pro—"

My hand twitched—not much, but slightly.

The cheese shifted suddenly—about two feet this time.

My hand sprang out, clawed at the mossy wall, and dragged me forward. I used my other hand to slow my progress, but when I looked back the cheese was once again on the move.

"What the heck is—"

I punched myself in the face. It wasn't that hard, but I wasn't expecting it. The blow smashed my crumbling nose and almost knocked me over.

Screaming in anger, I rallied back and gave my left arm such a slap that even the elbow flushed red.

Then the cheese went nuts. It must have

been pulled so hard on the wire that it actually took off into the air, flying away from me like a weird cheddar version of Superman.

My evil appendage backhanded me for good measure and then dug into the moss, dragging me along like a little kid pulls a new kite. I was ramming into walls, tripping over rocks, colliding with unseen trees growing from the path.

And, all the while, I'm thinking: *This is insane.*

The cheese shot up the spiraling steps of the Well, and I went after it. I couldn't help picturing a massive mousetrap waiting at the end of the wire to signal a hefty goodbye to what was left of my crumbling body.

Over the last few weeks, I'd really begun to understand the intense, arcane power of my rogue arm. As difficult as it was to believe that some of my fingers actually belonged to the devil himself, the strength with which I was dragged through the tunnel certainly made it seem like powerful magic was propelling me.

"Argghh!" I screamed as my head glanced off yet another rock, and then I was out—emerging from the top of the well into the dank, glistening tunnels of the subsewer.

I couldn't even see the cheese anymore; it was a distant memory.

Then it happened.

Crossing from the subsewer into one of the old subway tunnels, my demonic arm swung me around the bend with such force that my head smacked sharply off an ancient brick outcrop and I was immediately knocked unconscious.

I had one very quick and unusual dream

where I was riding an elephant with chronic diarrhea through a garden of enormous vegetables. Then I woke up . . .

. . . and soon wished I hadn't.

My head was still bouncing off something, and I was still being propelled along. But now I felt a cool carpet of grass passing underneath me. Somehow, my loss of consciousness had seen me through three different sets of tunnels and now I was back above ground, heading for—what?

I managed to glance up just in time to see the grim outline of Mortlake Church against the background of a dark night sky.

I could now see the cheese flying toward it, the wire dragging it so fast that it actually sprang up in places, ricocheting off rocks and losing parts of its mass in bushes and hedgerows along the way.

It wasn't even cheese-shaped any more. It closely resembled a slightly weatherbeaten block of butter.

I risked another glimpse forward, thinking at first that the entrance to the church was actually surrounded in flame. In fact, the flames were from torches carried by a large group of cloaked and hooded figures that gathered in a rough semicircle on the church steps. A little way behind them and slightly off to one side stood Max Moon and Jemini, both looking as worried as I felt.

Flames, said my ever-annoying subconscious. *They're going to burn you.*

But—seriously—what could I do? I quickly assessed my options. I came up with:

- Dig my good hand into the grass and get it ripped off.

- Dig my good hand and my legs into the grass and get them all ripped off.

- Dig my good hand and my legs into the grass, stop my progress, have a massive fight with my other hand—lose—and get ripped apart.

- Dig my good hand and my legs into the grass, stop my progress, have a massive fight with my other hand—win—and get burned alive by the town torch bearers.

- Wait and see what happens.

Guess which one I went for?

Trying to block out the weird chanting that I could now hear ringing clearly from the fast-approaching church entrance, I drew in a breath, thought of my friends, and prepared to take one for the team.

I could never have predicted what happened next. . . .

Screaming, rolling, and scraping to a halt, I found myself in the middle of the half-circle of mysterious chanters. I tried to read the expression on Max's face as my rogue hand dragged me to a standstill before the now stationary cheddar-ball.

The chanting stopped, and I noticed one of the cloaked figures at the edge of the semicircle letting go of the handle of a giant winch that must have been retracting the cheesewire.

I held my breath. My demonic hand suddenly sprang up like a cobra, hovering over the cheese almost as if it was in a sort of bizarre trance induced by really odd flute music.

It poised itself ready to strike and then, to my astonishment, proceeded to smash the cheese into oblivion. I mean, seriously smacking and punching that poor little ball until it had obliterated any sign of it, even to the point where it scratched at the last tiny smears on the church gravel.

I gulped back a confused, nervous glob of phlegm that felt like it might explode from my throat, and my hand relaxed, falling limp as if it had simply gone for a nap after a hard day's work.

One by one, all the hoods in the semicircle were drawn back, revealing many faces I recognized from Mortlake's undead community and a few that I definitely didn't.

While most of the group shuffled back, a tall, thin, and rather gaunt figure with sunken cheeks and a horrible squint stepped forward.

"Edward Robert Bagley," he began, and I knew it wasn't going to be good news because at that point I spotted Jemini tearing up and Max trying to comfort her. "You have been found guilty of being possessed by none other than the father of lies and evil destruction—the Satanic devil himself! And now, your sentence—"

The group suddenly went into a quick

huddle, accompanied by a lot of muttering and some very uncomfortable backward glances from the outer members.

Max was looking at me with a sad (but at least slightly supportive) grin, while Jemini had joined in the huddle and was arguing with the man I now thought of as Gaunt. I managed to catch the odd word, like "Edam" and "seriously?" but, apart from that, I just couldn't tell what was happening.

I looked down at my cursed hand and noticed for the first time that four of the fingers—the four fingers—were now considerably longer than the rest. They'd even grown elongated nails that tapered into points.

"Right," said a voice, and I looked up again.

Gaunt was now standing apart from the rest of the group, which had obviously come to a unanimous decision about my future.

"Edward Robert Bagley—"

"My middle name isn't Robert—"

"Shut up."

"Sorry."

"Ed Bagley—You Will Henceforth Be Taken From This Place And Flown To The Wilberforce Needlepinch Cheese Factory, Where His Satanic Foulness, The Devil Himself, Will Be Drawn From You In What Will Very Likely Become A Pitched Battle To The Death. You Will Be Accompanied By Mr. Moon And Miss Jemini, Who Have Taken A Blood Oath To Swear That Justice Will Be Done. Now—What Say You?"

I looked from Gaunt to Max and Jemini, and back again.

"Er . . . thanks?" I managed.

REASON...NOT TO FIGHT WITH THE UNDEAD:

THEY'VE GOT NOTHING TO LOSE

We stood on Inchfield Airstrip, a stretch of tarmac beside a really small hangar on the outskirts of Mortlake. I'd never seen a plane take off or land on the runway even when I was alive, so I found it hard to believe that the undead had some sort of regular flight plan going on. However, I found a lot difficult to believe these days, and Max Moon wasn't helping.

"It's like Superman with Kryptonite, or water for the Wicked Witch in *The Wizard of Oz*," he went on. "For the devil, it's—"

"Cheese?"

"Yeah. Big time."

I glared at him. "That's the most ridiculous thing I've ever heard in my life. For one thing, Kryptonite makes Superman really weak, whereas my hand smashed that cheese-ball into the stratosphere."

Jemini patted my shoulder and gave it a bit of a squeeze, causing a slightly awkward moment when one lump of flesh came away in her hand while another bit slapped wetly onto the tarmac.

"It's true, Ed," she said, rubbing her hands together and pretending to be cold when she actually just wanted to make sure she wasn't still holding some of my shoulder. "The devil really, really hates cheese. It's like the bane of his existence. One little piece—no problem, he can destroy it. But in a factory full of cheese?

He'd go crazy. And he might just come to the rescue of his missing fingers. I'm telling you, Ed—the devil absolutely cannot stand to be around cheese."

"It doesn't make any sense, though! Why?"

"No one really knows. It's a piece of ancient knowledge passed down among the elders of the undead community."

As the three of us stood there, slightly apart from the town council members, waiting for the plane to arrive, I tried to figure things out.

"So what you're saying is that all those people who go to church and pray on a Sunday should actually be praying at the cheese counter in the supermarket?"

Max sighed and nodded. "That's pretty much it," he said.

I turned to roll my eyes at him—and that's when I saw the flames among the trees.

There had to be twenty or thirty of them, all walking with a grim determination. Only a few carried torches—and I assumed they were not werewolves or vampires, considering the danger fire held for both groups. I could also see ghouls emerging from the undergrowth on the edge of the airfield, some scrambling like the fat babies beneath the graveyard, some walking upright like little imitations of children. All in all, it was a truly terrifying sight. Evil Clive's most solid support group had come out in force—and I couldn't really say that I blamed them.

The council stepped in front of us, their cloaks billowing in the evening breeze.

"Let me talk to them," I said, regretting the words almost as soon as they'd spilled from my lips. "After all, it's me they want."

The council leader I still thought of as Gaunt peered back at me twice before returning his attention to the treeline. "If you absolutely insist," was all he said, and the group parted slightly to allow me forward.

Max blocked my path.

"Don't do it, Ed," he muttered. "They'll rip you apart."

"He's right," Jemini echoed. "These people still believe you evicted Clive on purpose, and no amount of arcane testing or basic common sense will convince them otherwise. They'll stop at nothing to see you—Ed!"

I ignored the cries from my friends and marched determinedly across the tarmac. The army of darkness met me about halfway from the treeline, and a single thuggish-looking vampire stepped forward.

"You killed Evil Clive," he said simply.

I nodded but looked him straight in the eye. "I didn't mean to. The devil has taken control of my hand."

There was a series of mutterings among the members of the dark army, but the vampire shrugged.

"Either way, you're rotten to the core and we don't want you in Mortlake. You must be destroyed."

This time, I didn't nod or shake my head or even flinch. "The council has made its decision. Now, please—go home. I don't want anyone else to get hurt, and trust me, you will get hurt."

I looked along the line of vampires, werewolves, ghouls, and worse, noting several creatures I hadn't even seen at the town hall meeting. The basic body format of the undead community seemed to consist mostly of claws, fangs, and ghostly faces—but I'd also seen the odd freak of nature thrown into the bargain. One of the dark crew even looked like a mini eater.

I shuddered but managed to hold my ground.

"I'm going to face my punishment. I am really sorry about what happened to Clive. I know you might not believe me, but he was my friend too," I finished.

The vampire watched as I turned and walked at an even pace back toward the plane. Every part of me wanted to break into a run, but a voice deep inside my mind told me that everything was going to be okay.

I strode up to Gaunt and managed a weak smile.

"I think that went well."

The sallow-faced council leader glanced past me and said simply, "Get on the plane," but Max and Jemini were already grabbing my arms and propelling me forward.

Then all hell broke loose.

REASON...NOT TO FLY
UNDEAD AIRWAYS:
THE NAME SPEAKS FOR ITSELF

"What plane? It hasn't even—"

I turned and saw something shimmering on the airstrip in front of me. It looked like the offspring of a massive oblong coffin with wheels and a small plane, but it constantly flickered in and out of focus, as if it had only half a wing in real space.

I didn't have time to argue. As the army of hardcore Clive supporters poured through the trees, the plane door was flung open and a big, happy-looking Captain

Birdseye dude was standing in the opening, beckoning us all inside. He had a pair of empty eye sockets, but apart from that the whole scene would have made a nice TV commercial.

I scrambled up the single step that had slid down from the doorway and nearly fell as I climbed inside. Max and Jemini almost rolled over me.

"Welcome aboard," said the captain cheerily. "Just the three of you, is it? Great, I'll get us up and started."

He turned and sauntered off toward the front of the plane, flickering slightly as if he was in some sort of weird distortion of time.

"Arghghgh!"

Max and I both spun around to see Jemini literally crawling with ghouls. There were two attached to her arms, two on her legs, and one latched onto her midriff, all fastening their tiny teeth on any exposed flesh they could find.

The crowd of Clive supporters was attacking.

Max dashed over to help her but was driven back by a vampire and a werewolf, who both cannoned into him and sent him sprawling onto a row of seats.

"The door!" Jemini cried out. "Get the door!"

I cast a glance sideways, and before two more werewolves could dive through the hatch onto the plane, I immediately sprang into the accessway and pulled the door shut, driving the lock down with all my might.

I briefly considered peering out of the hatch window and making a face at them when the vampire who'd attacked Max snatched hold of my head and rammed it into the edge of one of the seats.

He looked moderately surprised when he realized that the rest of my body was still standing behind him.

Moving sharply, I bit his hand while instructing my corpse to give him a damn good kick in the back.

He spun around, letting go of my head in order to suck his wounded hand (either because he wanted to stop the blood flow or just because he was thirsty—I couldn't tell which).

My decapitated skull rolled off the seat and onto the floor, and I was just congratulating myself on my killer moves when the plane took off . . .

. . . and my head began to roll.

The deadplane hurtled down the runway at what felt like two hundred sixty miles an hour. From the outside, I don't doubt it looked like the world's

most sleek and sophisticated way to travel—
but inside, a lot of really bad stuff was happening.

Max furred up and punched the werewolf
he was fighting so hard that a tuft of hair flew
out of its face. The creature staggered slightly
and shoved Max into a secured control panel
on the wall of the plane.

"Can we just talk about this?" he yelled.

The werewolf snarled again and followed
up the assault with a savage punch, but Max
dodged aside and the furry fist went slamming
into the control panel, shattering the glass that
protected a long lever just below it.

Jemini was still screaming, but at least now she was fighting back. She shrugged off three ghouls and made a determined attack on another two, dropkicking one across the plane like a football while digging her fangs into the other as if it was the first course at a really good restaurant.

The ghouls immediately rallied. Scrambling around the plane like hungry spiders, they launched an attack on Max, helping his feral opponent no end.

When he finally hit the floor, the other werewolf ripped off the shattered cover of the control panel behind him and yanked on the lever.

The back of the plane began to open up in a wide yawn, and I noticed for the first time that my head was rolling toward the opening like a golf ball heading for the green. . . .

"Arghgh! Help yourself!" I yelled, but my body was a bit tied up with the vampire, who now had me in a Russian Death Grip—about the only wrestling move it's possible to do on an opponent who doesn't have a head.

I was in big trouble, even by my standards.

"Heeellllp!"

Jemini shrugged off the ghoul she'd been biting and hurtled for the aisle. But she ran too fast and actually dropkicked my head further toward the yawning touchline.

I rolled nose over cheek down the expanse, screaming like a five-year-old girl who's had her doll stolen.

"Ed!" Jemini put on a final burst of speed and dived over my escaping skull, using her last precious second to snatch hold of the backseat and reach out with her free hand.

I was seized from the wide and spiraling void of sky. Literally. I even felt the rush of wind on my face and saw the distant specks of figures fighting on the airfield below . . .

. . . and then I fainted.

A cascade of stars danced in front of my eyes and the world swam away. I had a strange and vivid dream about Mortlake, where the living and the undead all mingled together, as if one community was a beautiful painting and the other was a different picture on tracing paper which had simply been placed over the top. Both just walked around, living their various lives without ever knowing of the other community so close to them. It kinda made me sad, but not for long—because I woke up with a bang.

REASON...NOT TO WAKE UP:

THINGS MIGHT BE EVEN WORSE

You've seen it in a million movies. The brave hero gets into a really grim situation, then passes out and either wakes up in a hospital with lots of caring nurses tending to their wounds or on a feather bed in some magical kingdom surrounded by elves.

I lost consciousness as a decapitated head held in the hand of a screaming she-vampire at the tail end of a plane twisting through a vortex of rushing air. And then I woke up as a decapitated head held in the hand of a screaming she-vampire at the tail end of a plane twisting through a vortex of rushing air.

That's right, folks—I fainted for about eight seconds. Can anyone else say "pathetic"?

Jemini was still clinging to the last seat on the plane for dear death, while Max was taking on all five ghouls and the werewolf he'd been fighting in the first place.

Naturally, he was losing.

Time for action.

"Throw me!" I screamed at the top of my voice, hoping Jemini could hear me above the raging wind.

"What?"

came a distorted but frantic reply.

"THROW ME!"

"At who?"

"The werewolf!

"Are you crazy?"

"Max is in big trouble! Throw to kill!"

Jemini managed to drag herself round until she was clinging to the plane seat like a baby monkey clamped to its mother. Then she reeled back with her free arm and threw, pitched, hurled my decapitated head at the werewolf.

CRACK.

Getting a head butt is painful even when the person delivering the strike is about ten centimeters away from you. Getting a head

55

butt from thirty feet, well, that's kinda difficult to describe. It scores about a ten on the Painometer.

At least it did for wolf-boy. He flew back as if he'd been hit by a torpedo, smacked into the control panel, and slid down the wall with a gurgle. He must have caught the lever too because the back of the plane was slowly beginning to close up again.

"Max!" I screamed, bouncing off a row of seats and mashing my nose in a collision with one of the little square windows. "Get the ghouls out! Quick! Qui—"

My words were stifled as I rolled off the headrest and bumped onto the floor.

Still partially dazed from his bitter scrap with the rival wolf, Max had to use a chair to drag himself off his feet. Now fully wolfed up, he looked like a big carpet with teeth.

"Ghouls!" I reminded him. "Ghouls!"

It was then that I suddenly realized why my stomach hurt so much when I didn't actually have a stomach connected to my brain.

I squinted toward the cabin end of the aisle and saw my body being punched in the stomach by fang-boy.

Max Moon knew how painful ghoul bites could be—and he wasn't taking any chances. Leaping from seat to seat, he snatched up each fat baby and, as if he was handling hot coals, flung them down the aisle like some lunatic bowler at a ten-pin alley. One by one, the ghouls were disappearing into the fast-shrinking airstream with a variety of frantic, cackling cries of panic.

I reached out with my mind and finally made mental contact with my detached body. Fighting for control, I closed my eyes and imagined twisting out of the vampire's grip and dropkicking him toward the back of the plane.

I opened my eyes—and couldn't help but feel a little disappointed.

The good news was that my body had twisted out of the vampire's grip.

The bad news was that I was now punching the stuffing out of one of the plane seats while my opponent took a moment to get his breath and snicker behind my back.

I gritted my teeth and tried again.

This time, my body met the vampire's attack with a sharp elbow that sprang up and caught him square on the jawline and sent him crashing to the floor.

Ha! He wasn't expecting that.

Max Moon was nearing the last level of what had quickly become the National Ghoul-Tossing Challenge. With a final, thunderous bellow of rage, he hurled the last fat baby at the thin sliver of daylight that still remained visible between the closing jaws of the plane's tail end.

The body was sucked through the gap, and the last thing anyone saw was a chubby little face with a vaguely contorted expression.

I can't stand ghouls.

When the tail closed, Jemini let go of the backseat and collapsed in a heap.

"Argh!"

The cry came from Max, who was going toe to toe with the incensed werewolf. Incredibly, it had recovered from my awesome head butt and was lifting Max over his shoulders, preparing to deliver some sort of airborne power slam.

Jemini rolled onto her feet and flew down the aisle like a swooping eagle, landing on the werewolf in a fury of vampiric fangs and claws. The wolf dropped Max and the three of them rolled away into one corner of the plane, looking like a cartoon fight ball with arms and legs appearing and disappearing at random.

I was concentrating on other things.

Using every tiny section of mind power I could summon, I ordered, instructed, commanded my body to come and fetch my head.

It spun around, delivered two quick punches that actually winded the vampire—and began to stagger quickly in my direction.

There was a brief moment of terror as one of my own feet nearly stamped off my nose, and then I was lifted carefully onto my shoulders.

I concentrated hard until the soft, wet, sickly sucking sound indicated that I was reattached.

Now it was stomping time.

I spun around just as the vampire careered into me, but two swift knee lifts had him thinking twice. I snatched hold of his throat with my demonic hand, hoping it would do something pretty awesome of its own accord.

It didn't.

The vampire looked down at the clasp,

realized there wasn't much behind it, and broke the hold, scooping me up like a rag doll and tossing me aside.

I hit the wall of the plane and fell awkwardly between two rows of seats, groaning as three of my fingers rolled under one of them.

Jemini leaped onto the vampire's back, sinking her fangs into his neck and ripping great clumps of his hair out in fistfuls.

Screaming with rage, the vampire threw himself back and tried to ram her against the wall, but Jemini was too quick for him. She evaded the strike and slammed the side of her hand into the vampire's throat.

It clawed ineffectually at the sudden exhalation of breath and collapsed into unconsciousness. Jemini fell onto her knees beside it, shaking her head to steady herself.

"Good move!" I cried, still hunting around on the floor for my fingers.

Max ducked two strikes from the were-wolf and gouged a vicious wound in its side. Then he snatched hold of the wolf's face and dragged it down, driving his kneecap into its forehead.

It twitched a few times and then fell into a deep, dark slumber.

Max and Jemini both clambered to their feet while I used the plane seats to haul myself into a vaguely upright position.

The plane looked as though a bomb had gone off inside it.

To my astonishment, as the three of us fought to gain some sort of composure, the cabin door opened and the captain strode out with a pleasant and somewhat detached smile on his face.

"Thank you for flying today," he said, opening his arms widely and pointing in all directions. "The exits are here and here. Under your seats, you will find a safety vest which you can inflate by blowing into the small tube at the top. Once again, thank you for flying Deadspace Airlines."

He beamed one last smile at us and headed back into the cockpit, closing the cabin door gently behind him.

I turned to look at Jemini and Max, who were also covered in blood. "What is wrong with that guy?"

Max shrugged. "He's on a loop. That's what deadspace is—it just goes round and round. Just be grateful you didn't become a phantom."

Grateful.

I looked down at myself and grimaced.

"I'm not grateful for having the devil's fingers! What's the point of having an ultra-powerful demonic hand that only fights when it wants to?"

I slumped into one of the seats, curled up against the wall, and prayed for sleep.

REASON...NOT TO FLY
DEADSPACE AIRLINES:
THEY DON'T STOP

When I woke up this time, all was calm and peaceful. It's a pity I was stuck to the leather of the seat by a smelly glue that seemed to consist largely of my own spit, but you can't have everything.

The deadplane was hurtling along at breakneck speed, but it was also making practically no noise. For some reason, that fact really unnerved me. However, it was nothing compared to the stress from my conversation with Jemini.

"Say that again?" I gasped. "What do you

mean, we're not landing?" I was looking out of the window onto a thick carpet of forest that rushed past below us at an impossible speed. "We're just above the treeline; we have to be landing."

"This plane only takes off and lands at Inchfield," Jemini explained. "Apart from that, it goes in a circle around the world. It's like a video that just keeps on playing—we're lucky it's even solid enough to fly in, really."

I didn't even want to guess what she meant by that, so I just nodded. "So how do we get off?"

"We jump."

"What? We're going at two hundred miles an hour or something!"

"Oh, get over it, Ed," Max laughed. "Seriously, it's such a rush! I'll just crash through the trees, Jemini will fly to the ground and—"

"I'll fall to pieces?"

"Well, yeah . . . but only like you always do. Besides, you'll put yourself back together again."

"Don't worry, Ed," Jemini said, giving me another of her mini-squeezes, "we're right behind you."

Max made a face that indicated he was

about to do something crazy and bolted over to the plane doors.

"Max—"

"You only die once, Ed ," he cackled, sliding down the lock and throwing open the portal so that a whirlwind blast of air almost ripped it off the plane.

Then he was gone.

Yep—the big furball jumped. Just like that.

I turned to make some sort of stunned remark to Jemini, but she rose into the air and followed after him.

If you don't jump now, said the nagging little voice in my head, *they'll be MILES away by the time you land.*

I gulped back a tiny piece of vomit that had risen in my throat, closed my eyes, and ran straight into the wall next to the open doorway.

"Owww! Damn it!"

I staggered back, holding my nose, and got sucked through the hole anyway. . . .

"Aaaaaaaaaaaaarggghhhhh!"

Some people say you haven't lived until you've jumped out of a plane and seen the earth screaming toward you a million billion miles an hour.

I hate those people.

REASON...NOT TO LAND IN A FOREST FACE-FIRST:

IT HURTS

The air hit me like a tidal wave of pure, chaotic energy.

My hand snapped back and flew off into the wind.

I gritted my teeth, waiting for my head to rip apart from my neck and follow it. Thankfully, this time it stayed put, unlike my right leg, my left ear, at least half the body fat on my belly, and something I didn't even realize I had until it exploded out of my mouth and shot away.

I would have sobbed, I would have cried,

I would have yelled out in total misery and despair if I hadn't crashed through the forest roof at that point.

I swear to this day that I hit every single branch of the massive, ugly, rotten tree I landed in. But the absolutely worst thing that happened to me during my whole afterlife happened as I hit the lowest branch: a twig went straight through my right eye, and it popped like a fat pimple.

My head snapped back with the pain and a sickness came rushing over me. I wriggled off the branch and fell about twenty feet, half splashing, half thumping into a dirty puddle at the foot of the tree.

I yelped and rolled over, forgetting that I had a leg missing and trying but failing to stand on the remaining one.

Cursing everything I could think of, I glanced up to see my eyeball stuck on the end of the lowest branch like a cherry on a stick.

"You okay, buddy?"

The voice was unmistakably Max's, and I squirmed around to face him.

"Do I look okay?" I snapped, getting even angrier when it became apparent that Max was completely unscathed apart from a sparse covering of leaves and other forest foliage. "I mean, seriously—no leg, no good hand, half my flesh missing, and my former eyeball wedged up there." I pointed with one of my non-devil fingers. "Would you be okay?"

Jemini appeared from between two trees a little way down the path. If anything, she was even less disheveled than Max.

"Clive could see quite well with two empty sockets," she said with a shrug. "Are you sure you actually need your eyes?"

I was about to hurl a raft of abuse back at her when I tried closing my left eye tightly and realized that I could actually see quite clearly from the empty socket. If anything, the world was in slightly sharper focus but in a very fine blue haze.

However, it was the principle of the thing.

"I know it's greedy," I muttered, "but I really would like my other eyeball back—so if you can both just hang there for a second, I'll lie down here and concentrate on remote-calling all my missing body parts, thank you so very much."

REASON ...TO RUN FROM LOUD NOISES IN THE FOREST:

EVERYTHING IN THERE WANTS TO EAT YOUR FACE

A heavy rain was soaking through the trees as we squelched along the forest path. In fact, squelching wasn't really what we were doing at all. We were all running as if the hounds of hell were after us. For all I knew, they were.

A series of loud and terrifyingly pitched howls had erupted all over the forest, and the way I looked at it, if a werewolf and a vampire suddenly both broke into a run, it's probably a fair bet the thing behind you doesn't do weekend shifts at Disney World.

Still, I was feeling slightly better. Despite the fact that Jemini told me my body's re-forming was the most disgusting thing she'd ever seen, my mood was actually beginning to pick up. Sure, I'd made enemies in Mort-lake, but at least I hadn't been banished by the council. When it came right down to it, I had a chance to fight the devil in a cheese factory, which—according to Max—was like a team of Little Leaguers playing the Green Bay Packers in the Amazon basin.

"Where are we, anyway?" I asked, trying not to sound as happy as I felt.

"Harmfield," Max growled, wringing some rainwater from his fur. "We're just crossing the border from Westwood. The cheese factory is about two minutes away."

"The Wilberforce Needlepinch Cheese Factory," Jemini corrected him.

We trudged on through the rain.

"Who is Wilberforce Needlepinch, anyway?"

Jemini and Max shared one of those glances that reminded me they'd both been undead a lot longer than I had.

"He was just an old guy who owned the factory," Max muttered. "He died a long time ago."

I nodded and waited a few seconds to let the pair of them relax. Then I grinned and said, "So why did you just look at each other in that weird, freaked-out way?"

Jemini sighed.

"Well, let's just say that Kambo Cheapteeth wasn't the only man ever to do a deal with the devil. Needlepinch was another one who went down that path, and when he died—something horrible happened to him, something that only happens to people who did some really bad stuff during their lives."

"What was that?"

"He became a Host."

I waited for more information, but both Max and Jemini were shuddering.

"I'm guessing you don't mean like a game-show host?"

"A Host is a person whose soul gets imprisoned and transformed at the same time."

"Imprisoned and transformed into what?"

The rain was getting heavier now and we found ourselves slipping and sliding through the trees on a sort of downward slalom. When we had finally all crashed, skidded, and staggered from the edge of the forest, Jemini stuck up her hand and pointed with a single, shaking finger.

"Into that," she finished.

Max and I both gulped.

There, on a low hill beside the edge of the forest, was the ugliest, most sprawling, and impossibly massive building I had ever seen in my life. Its many spiny turrets, buttresses, and crenellations made it look like a massive, spiky-haired face, while the hundreds of shattered windows reminded me of row upon row of gnarled, jagged teeth.

"So," I said, trying to keep my voice steady, "what you're saying is that the Wilberforce Needlepinch Cheese Factory is actually . . . Wilberforce Needlepinch himself."

As if to illustrate the point, a streak of lightning suddenly lit up the entire expanse of countryside.

I was about to point out how eerie it made the building look when a second bolt hit me directly on the forehead, frying my skin like a side of fatty bacon . . .

Max leaped ten feet into the air.

Jemini screamed.

I just smiled faintly and fell over backward.

REASON...NOT TO GET HIT BY LIGHTNING:

IT HURTS

Since I'd joined the elite but kinda crummy membership of the walking, talking dead, physical pain had become second nature to me.

If you poke me in the eye, it doesn't really hurt—it just stings, smarts, and squelches a bit.

If you pull my arm off, it doesn't really hurt—it just burns like a demon and aches like crazy.

Being scratched, torn, and ripped apart by

tiny flying imps was a complete bummer, I have to admit.

But being electrocuted and burned, flayed and melted by a huge bolt of pure energy was still right up there at number one.

I screamed so hard my lungs felt like they were going to explode. Max rolled me up and down the hillside, and Jemini—for reasons best known to herself—kicked me in the face a few times (to "stamp out the flames," she said).

When I finally staggered back to my feet, I felt like an ant squashed on the bottom of a giant's shoe, and I looked like a pork rind.

"Argghhghh—the pain!"

"Breathe, Ed!"

"Yeah—just breathe!"

"Ahhhhhhh!"

I held my breath and tried to wish away

the agony. It seemed to work . . . and within a few seconds we were all up and walking again, heading for the great looming evil that was the factory.

The rain poured on—and the conversation was just as depressing.

"Does it look really bad?" I asked, trying to ignore the smell of fried chicken.

"No, buddy."

"Not at all, Ed—you look fine. Ha! I'd still go out with you on a date. . . ."

I glanced sideways at her, but she was doing a good job of not snickering.

Max whistled between his teeth. "Seriously. We wouldn't lie to you. It's not that bad. Personally, though, I'd steer away from mirrors for the time being."

And that's when I knew the truth. I could have gone on a date with a girl made entirely of elephant snot and she would have been the looker.

If the Wilberforce Needlepinch Cheese Factory looked ugly from a distance, up close it was a real eyesore. The front doors were hanging off their hinges, both covered in some weird algae that had also mutated much of the brickwork on either side.

It was truly a hideous sight, but I had no real choice but to go in. Otherwise, where could I go? The world of the newly undead was alien to me. Sure, I could return to a mob of haters in Mortlake . . . but what if I went back a hero? A zombie who'd fought the devil and won? After all, if I didn't win I didn't have to worry about going anywhere ever again.

Besides, Jemini and Max had taken a blood oath to ensure that justice would be done. Whatever that meant. I was just really lucky I had friends willing—quite literally—to put their necks on the line to support me.

Gulp.

I returned my attention to Wilberforce Needlepinch's grim creation.

There were no lights inside the building

and leaves swirled up around the entrance, whipped by some sort of minor vortex that nestled inside the main passage. To finish off the grisly picture, it seemed as if half the actual building was missing, demolished perhaps by a fighter plane during the war or even by some natural disaster.

Looking at the monstrosity, there was only one statement I felt inclined to make.

"Who'd buy cheese from here? Even a deranged mouse with no sense of smell would bolt past it at a hundred miles an hour."

Jemini rolled her eyes. "How many times do we have to go through this, Ed? We interact with the spirit of buildings—that's why you never see kids in Mortlake School or people in the street. I can assure you that it doesn't look like this to the breathers. It is a working factory. There's enough cheese in there to kill a mouse the size of a dinosaur."

I nodded reluctantly and we ventured up the stairs, beyond the giant entrance doors, and into the main hall.

If the undead really did see only the souls of buildings, then Wilberforce Needlepinch had been rotten to the core. His cheese factory was absolutely putrid.

Now, here's a fact: cheese smells. I'm not talking about your great-aunt's ear-cheese, either—I'm talking about the normal, everyday stuff. If you leave cheese on a kitchen counter long enough, it will actually follow you to work in the morning.

The Wilberforce Needlepinch Cheese Factory stank beyond imagination.

The hallway yawned widely ahead of us, and an eerie, twittering sound was now clearly audible in the gloom.

Something was crawling on the walls. At first, I took it for a shadow or the wind bothering the moss, but now, as we moved on down the hall, I could see there was definitely a carpet of tiny, odd misshapen insects trailing our progress. They moved in a bizarre formation, almost like an arranged attack unit, zigzagging through the myriad network of cracks in the wall pattern.

"Hate this place already," Max muttered.

I shuddered in agreement.

The three of us arrived at a fork, and we instinctively looked to Jemini for guidance.

"Which way?"

"I'm not sure," she said, sniffing the air. "But the smell of cheese is strongest that way."

We turned right and headed down a new hallway with whitewashed walls and a creepy tiled floor that reflected our own images back at us. I don't know what surprised me more—that Jemini had a reflection or that this part of the floor was clean enough to see it in.

At another split, we all turned left—and stopped dead.

In front of us was a dead end, but the blocking wall contained an enormous painting lit by a strange and unnaturally pale light.

The picture was of a short but very fat old man in what looked like a doctor's lab coat.

He had sagging jowls and a greenish tinge to his skin, and he wore a pair of tiny circular glasses. The picture was odd, and something about the way the old man was gleefully rubbing his hands together really gave me the creeps. Looking over at Max and Jemini, I could see they felt the same way.

"Wilberforce Needlepinch," Max muttered. "Has to be, doesn't it?"

"Let's turn back," Jemini said, smiling uncomfortably and leading both of us away by the elbows.

All three of us kept looking back.

We soon rounded yet another corner in the endless maze of passages, but this time, the cheese smell grew really strong.

My hand began to twitch.

REASON...NOT TO SUMMON THE DEVIL:

HE'S THE DEVIL

My hand flew up suddenly and slapped onto the wall like a wet fish hitting a cutting board. Max and Jemini both leaped back as my four demonic fingers dug into the plaster and began to wrench me forward at an alarming rate.

"Arghgh! Here we go again! Argghhh!" I cried.

I was dragged up the hallway, cata-pulted through a set of swinging doors that looked like they should have been guarding an emergency room at the hospital, and driven headfirst down a new passageway that, to me, smelled more of disinfectant than cheese.

"Help me! Arghgh! Hold me back or something! Help! HELP!"

I managed to throw myself onto the floor and wedged both feet against the wall so that my rogue limb was forced to pull my entire weight forward.

It did. Despite straining every muscle and sinew in my rapidly decomposing body, I couldn't stop myself from slowly inching away once again.

"Max!" I screamed at the top of my lungs. "Jemini! Where are you two?"

I twisted around on the floor, trying to see between my own legs as I was hauled off toward the far end of the corridor.

Max and Jemini were both following me, but neither was in any particular rush. In fact, Max looked like he was taking an early afternoon stroll in an old lady's garden!

"Help! What's wrong with you?"

Max shrugged his shoulders.

"We can't, Ed," he called out. "It's the rule of the council. You've got to do this on your own. I kno—"

"Sorry, Ed," Jemini interrupted. "We can only intervene once the demon is out of the box, so to speak. Good luck, though!"

Good luck? Was she kidding!

My demonic limb was now firmly in control, spinning me around on the tiled floor and rushing me toward yet another set of heavy doors at the end of the hall.

I smashed open the doors like a human-sized battering ram and flipped over twice before skidding, scrambling, and sliding to a standstill in a room twice the size of a cathedral.

Max and Jemini spilled into the vast chamber behind me, both primed and ready for some sort of explosive confrontation.

My hand was now going nova, the four fingers twitching, scratching, and even snapping at the other five in some sort of spider-like duel.

But at least I wasn't still being pulled along the floor. And suddenly I saw why.

The columns I had taken to be rows and rows of pillars holding up the ceiling of the room were actually stacks of cheese. They rose higher than the surrounding walls, which I could now see were also blocks of cheese piled in miniature obelisks all along the back half of the room.

The place smelled baaaaaad.

My hand snapped back and forth, rising up like a cobra and slowly turning three hundred sixty degrees as it felt the incredible presence of so much dairy goodness.

Then it happened.

First my hand punched the floor, driving me onto my knees and slamming the fist down . . .

Once.

Twice.

Three times.

Then there was a sickening, severing, scorching sound, and a tiny line of blood ripped across the knuckles between the back of my hand and the four possessed fingers.

"Argghh!" I screamed, clutching at the hand and holding it down as blood and bone began to ooze out.

The fingers twisted and turned as they scrambled to escape, leaving torn and jagged wounds behind them.

And then, heaving back on my hand with a spitting hiss at the escaping digits, I watched helplessly as the fingers shot across the floor like insane worms toward the biggest cheese stack.

"You're free of him, Ed!" Jemini cried from just inside the doorway, with Max baying behind her.

"Run, buddy! Run!"

I turned tail and tried to flee, but a dark and terrible cackle echoed around the vast room. The swing doors slammed shut and a network of moss immediately grew over them.

"Do you really think it would be that easy?" said a loud, menacing voice like thick syrup. "Did you truly believe that you could trespass on my property without a reckoning?"

To this day, I really wish I hadn't looked up. I still don't know why I did. I guess something in the corner of my vision told me things weren't right.

Very close to the ceiling of the immense hall, a network of ventilation grids provided a fresh flow of air to the cheesemakers.

Today they were providing a new tide of the weird insects I'd seen earlier. They swept out of the grid and swarmed across the ceiling, moving in one long, bleeding shadow that made it look as though an impossibly dark cloud was passing overhead.

I swallowed back a gulp of fear and spun around, determined to find another way out of the room.

Unfortunately, I ran into big trouble.

The four finger worms had made a bee-line for the largest tower of cheese and had burrowed straight into it, bringing the entire stack down on top of them. The debris of so much fresh cheese was too much for the fingers to take, so they had shot back out of the pile and were writhing weakly on a tiny cheese-free scrap of floor at the end of the hall.

"Stamp on them," Max yelled, his attention split between the hunt for an escape route and the trillion insects advancing overhead.

"Leave it, Ed!" The counterwarning came from Jemini, who had overtaken the two of us and was throwing big lumps of cheese off a table she'd decided might be blocking the route to freedom.

I really wanted to leave those fingers alone, honestly, I did. But the memory of what they made me do to Evil Clive rose inside my head and I just couldn't help myself.

Screaming with rage, I took a run up and leaped into the air, landing with a half-skid among the finger worms.

"Take this, you stubby little freaks!" I screamed, stomping and stamping every square inch of the ground while the pudgy digits snaked and slithered around my boots.

And then a massive, thunderous avalanche of sound exploded behind me.

"The wall!" Max boomed. "The wall is moving! Look!"

Sure enough, one entire side of the room was crunching forward, crushing tables, chairs, and a mountain of cheese on its path toward us. Worse still, a series of bizarre cracks and holes had scarred the surface of the wall, turning it into a warped and twisted face that I just knew belonged to the reckless soul of Wilberforce Needlepinch.

"Ed! Eddddd!" Jemini had finished heaving aside blocks of the cheese but was now staring wide-eyed in my direction.

I gaped at her.

"What is it? What's wron—"

A flash of green whooshed beneath my feet and slowly I turned around.

The four fingers had knitted together across a strip of thin flesh that was, very slowly, growing a large and demonic-looking crimson hand.

The devil.

I took several steps back . . .

. . . crashed into Max . . .

. . . and the insects began to rain down upon us.

REASON...TO HATE INSECTS:

THEY HAVE MORE LEGS THAN TEETH, AND THAT'S JUST WRONG

Max and I were rolling around on the floor, clawing at our own faces and spitting out great mouthfuls of the teeming, streaming mass of shiny black insects. The chittering critters were everywhere. I was scooping them out of my nose, my ears, and even my eye sockets.

If anything, the attack on Max was worse. I couldn't even see my friend anymore. He was just a great big furry cocoon, wrapped in tiny, shiny, black shells.

The wall continued to rumble, crushing everything in its path and rapidly shrinking the room.

Jemini rose quickly into the air, soaring toward us at her top speed.

Fangs and claws elongating, she reached down and slashed two swathes of the insects out of Max's fur. She took hold of the exposed fur in her fists and rose into the air, pulling Max up with her.

"Shake yourself, Max! C'mon! All dogs can do that!"

Max wriggled around inside the swarm, slowly shedding shower after shower of the insects onto the factory floor.

I vomited up a throatful of insects and yelled out for help.

Jemini quickly zoomed to my rescue, but she never made it.

A massive clawed hand, gleaming red and wreathed in flame, snatched her out of the air and hurled her against the wall as if she was a puppy's chew toy. She hit the brickwork and plummeted to the ground.

There was a grim rumble of earsplitting laughter, and the hand swept back toward me.

I wriggled and squirmed in the wild mass of insects, spinning myself around on the floor and trying desperately to bite down on anything crunchy that ventured beyond my lips, but I had other problems. . . .

The devil's hand closed around my legs and hauled me into the air, shaking me free of the insects and holding me upside down over the shrinking expanse of the great cheese hall.

Seeing the devil for the first time is a truly sobering experience. I'll be honest, though; seeing him upside down wasn't actually that bad. I think I would have been a lot more terrified had he held me the right side up.

He roared like a mountain lion, and I

gagged as he hit me with the most revolting breath I'd ever smelled. I might have even thrown up a little in my mouth.

"ED . . . BAGLEY," came the booming voice.

I caught an image of charred, burning skin, missing tufts of hair, and melted face—then realized that there was a mirror on the moving wall of the factory and I was actually looking at a reflection of myself. As I watched, the reflection changed—and I saw Evil Clive.

Then it happened. Suddenly, the factory, the grim shadow hanging over me, even my friends, all disappeared. . . .

I was sitting in a white room on a really comfortable sofa. Sitting across from me, on an equally fluffy red armchair, was Evil Clive. He was exactly the way I remembered him, right down to the evil grin and the backward Dead Donkey baseball cap.

I gulped. "C-Clive?"

The skeleton nodded. "Hey, Ed. How's it going?"

"F-fine," I managed. "I-I'm dreaming, right?"

"Yes, you are."

"Did I die?"

"No . . . you fainted. Don't feel bad about that. You've just seen the devil in the flesh and your mind can't cope with it. But you know what they say: anything that doesn't kill us makes us stronger."

I nodded slowly, taking in the general whiteness of my surroundings.

I gulped again. "Er, will I be going back soon?"

"Yes," said Clive with a friendly nod. "And when you do, remember this: nothing is ever as bad as it looks. Okay?"

I smiled weakly. "Yeah. Okay."

"Good. Off you go, then."

I felt the room begin to swim around me. I guess I was waking up.

"C-Clive!" I shouted into the receding glimmer of the dream.

"Yeah?"

"I'm sorry about . . . evicting you."

The skeleton's grin loomed out of the blinding light, and the voice behind it muttered, "Kid—don't sweat the small stuff."

I awoke, cold and sharp.

Fighting to see my real surroundings, I craned my neck up again and immediately wished I hadn't.

The devil was massive.

I'm going to say that again, just so you fully understand.

The devil was massive, and I'm not talking about the size of that big kid in school who keeps getting suspended for beating up the teachers. I'm talking two-story-house massive.

If you've ever seen movies or documentaries about the Greek myths, then you'll know what a Minotaur looks like: a great hulking bull on two legs with muscles rippling through every limb. The devil is basically a very big version of that. The horns weren't entirely unexpected, but I'd always thought they would point up, not down. The nose ring was a shock, because I never realized the devil would keep up with fashion and stuff.

Still, you get the picture.

Monster.

"ED . . . BAGLEY," he said again.

I tried to stop choking and sniveling long enough to see what was happening in the room.

The wall had stopped rolling forward and was now extending rows of sharp spikes from every corner. Evidently, Wilberforce Needle-pinch was going to make sure his infernal master's chosen victims weren't going to escape anytime soon. . . .

I twisted and tried to kick out of the devil's grip, but he lifted me even higher. Now I was face-to-face with the jaws of doom, and the smell was indescribable.

"You dare to challenge me, Ed Bagley? Me—who could crush you in a heartbeat?"

The world turned upside down once again and I found myself held right side up in the devil's fist. I couldn't move.

Revealed in all its glory, the face of the beast was truly terrifying to behold, and I could actually feel the flaming yellow eyes burning what remained of the skin on my face.

"You destroyed Kambo Cheapteeth, one of my very favorites—and even the sacrifice of that skeletal loser you slaughtered cannot make up for that."

"You did that through me!" I managed.

I gritted my teeth and tried to pour every ounce of strength into my arm muscles, but the grip was like iron.

"And now, Ed Bagley, your own time has finally come. Prepare to be destroyed."

The pain started as a dull throb, regular but all over my body in small bursts, a low, burning ache that slowly intensified. I looked down and saw flames begin to spring from between the giant fingers. I was on fire . . . I was going to burn into dust.

Max sprang to his feet and charged, digging his claws into the devil's chunky red legs and taking a big, enormous, savage werewolf bite.

The devil flinched and kicked out, smashing Max through the side wall of the factory. He landed on a hillside in the pouring rain, and I could see him trying and failing to get back to his feet.

That's when the hopelessness set in, and I stopped struggling to free myself from the grip still pinning me to the wall. A kind of weary haze tumbled over me, and I closed my tired eyes.

This is the devil. What chance can we possibly have of surviving?

Jemini had shaken off her insect coat and was back in action. Grabbing a heavy wooden leg off a half-destroyed table, she was now battering away at the struts supporting one of the giant cheese vats at the back of the room.

CRUNCH.

The vat gave a monstrous, creaking sigh and hit the tiles with a bang, spewing soft, molten cheese across the factory floor. The dairy river rolled over all the floor cracks and quickly became a tide of cheesy goodness.

Jemini staggered back from the vat, bleeding and exhausted but very pleased with herself.

The devil screamed and twitched, waking

me from my defeated, dreamy state. The great beast's cloven-hoofed feet were now covered in an ocean of sticky cheese and had begun to smoke and hiss. I squirmed, wriggled, shimmied, and snaked my way under the fingers and dropped, tumbling head over heels, into the splashing river of molten cheese.

The devil bellowed with rage and ripped his hooves free from the sticky mass.

I hit the surface of what was now basically a cheese 'n' insect soup and flipped myself onto my back, just in time to dodge the massive hoof that came slamming down inches from where I'd just landed. I dodged right, scrambled to my feet, and leaped sideways.

The hoof came down again like a crack of thunder, but this time it split the tiles and splashed cheese and insects in every direction. It would have flattened me like a pan-cake if I'd still been lying there.

"Out!" I screamed at Jemini, who was still fighting to get to her feet through the sticky cheese soup that covered the floor. "Out!"

Then I turned and bolted for the hole in

the wall that Max had been hurled through.

The devil charged after me.

"Arrghghh!"

I slipped in the goo, landed flatly on my side, and gagged. The cheese stank worse than ever.

"Go, Ed! Go!"

Jemini had flown in front of the devil and was clawing ineffectually at his enormous face while he tried to swat her away like a fly.

Following her instructions, I spun on my heel and ran like the wind, or at least like the wind would run if it had the devil after it.

I leapfrogged a medium-sized mountain of packaged cheese and made for the hole. As I ran, Wilberforce Needlepinch decided to cut me off, driving his spiked wall forward with incredible force.

"Arghghghnnnnooooooooooooooo!"

The scream came from Jemini, who'd been snatched up and hurled by the devil. She rocketed over my head and disappeared through the hole, bouncing over the hillside in a weird series of fits and bursts.

Please let her be okay, I thought. *She's only here because of me. I guess at least she's out of the factory.*

That's when a last-minute plan occurred to me. A plan so crazy that even a half-deranged mutant elephant wouldn't have tried it.

That didn't stop me.

I skidded on the river of cheese and surfed my way in a complete arc until I was face-to-face with the devil once more. I shot forward, running with everything I had, and flattened myself out and slid between the red giant's two great legs.

Then, amid the beast's sudden confusion, I greeted the onrushing wall of spikes with open arms, took hold of two of them, and began to climb. Blood sprayed from my rotting hands as I progressed up the moving wall, yelping in pain as the spikes

bit into me.
When I reached
the middle of
the wall, I must
have looked like
a shish kabob.

Partly aston-
ished and partly
bemused, the devil
turned this way and that,
peering all around the factory floor before he thought
to cast a glance up at the
shifting wall.

"Yeah," I cried, scream-
ing out the word with
every burst of breath I still
had in me, "here I am, you

hoof-trottered, hairy-legged, cow-headed moron."

The devil's eyes gleamed with sudden fire.

"You dare to—"

"Yes I dare! No wonder you live in the underworld, you great ugly monster! I've seen dog turds that look better than you!"

"You will d—"

"Even your horns are lame, you moose-faced sack of dried camel vomit!"

"Argghghh!" The devil boomed, shaking

the foundations of the factory. "ROAOOOO-OOOOOOOOOR!"

His hot, stinking breath exploded through my hair and nostrils.

"Is that all you've got, you mud-licking Minotaur wannabe? No wonder Evil Clive scared you. What did he do, show you a mirror?"

Now the eyes were blazing like twin furnaces, and every muscle on the bulbous arms was wrestling every vein for control of the explosion of strength that was brewing.

"EDDDDDDDDD…BAGGGGGGGLEY—"

I rolled my eyes.

"Yeah, yeah. Do your worst! Come over here, and I'll kick your stinkin' teeth in!"

The devil charged.

Flames burst from his hooves with every step, and it hurtled toward me with all its spite and anger, rage pouring from every orifice and spit flying from the corners of its stench-ridden mouth.

As if detecting what I was about to do, the soul of Wilberforce Needlepinch desperately tried to stop the wall from moving forward, inching back with what must have been phenomenal mental effort.

Sadly, it was too little too late.

I jumped down and slid forward beneath the devil's legs and spun around to watch it crash into the wall of deadly spikes.

The soul of Wilberforce Needlepinch cried out in warning.

"Arghghghghgghghghghghghgh!"

There was a sickening thud, a squelching sound, and an eye-watering waft of stink . . .

And then there was silence.

I staggered to my feet, dragged myself forward, and half stumbled, half fell over the pile of packaged cheese that blocked my way to the hole in the side of the factory wall.

Then, putting in as much of a determined effort as I could muster, I began very slowly to ascend the mountain. I tumbled back every few steps, but that didn't stop me, and I persevered, hauling my devastated body toward the gap and my freedom.

Finally, reaching the edge of the hole, I looked out onto the rainy hillside, just able to make out the two tattered shapes that were my two best friends, and a tired smile split my cracked and shattered lips.

I'd made it. I had finally defeated the devil and—

"ED BAGLEY."

I turned around—and, this time, I very nearly cried.

REASON ... NEVER TO COUNT THE DEVIL OUT:

DIDN'T YOU HEAR ME LAST TIME? HE'S THE DEVIL!

A shimmer of greenish-golden energy was bleeding from the giant creature speared to the factory wall. A separate, arcane strand of the same magic was seeping from the wall itself—and both were meeting in the middle.

I was so, so tired of fighting. I actually didn't think I had any more strength left to give. I wanted to run, but something about the weaving lines of energy grabbed my attention and simply wouldn't let go.

I gulped.

The two pulsing colors melted together and began to form into two separate human-oid shapes. One was short and round, the other tall and thin. One had flabby jowls and tiny circular glasses, the other swept, jet-black hair and a triangular goatee.

I took a deep breath as the shapes completed their transmogrification.

A series of grim cackles filled the room, but these seemed to come from the very walls—either that or from the millions of tiny, chittering insects that littered the floor, all drowning in a lake of melted cheese.

The two figures on the factory floor were now clearly defined and very visible.

One was unmistakably Wilberforce Needlepinch. The other, I had to assume, was the human manifestation of the devil himself.

I took a deep breath and bunched both my fists into balls.

"Wow," I said loudly, looking down on them both from my lofty perch. "I admit I'm shocked. I really didn't think you two could get any uglier. . . ."

Then I turned around.

And I really, really, really ran.

REASON...TO RUN AWAY FROM A SECOND FIGHT WITH THE DEVIL:

YOU'RE JUST NOT LISTENING, ~~ARE YOU?~~

I felt like Indiana Jones in the first part of *Raiders of the Lost Ark*. I was running toward Max and Jemini, waving my arms, and they were jumping up and down with glee because they thought everything was fine.

It was only when I got close enough for them to read my tortured expression that they both realized I was still in a ton of trouble.

The rain hammered the hillside, turning

every muddy puddle into a deadly patch of quicksand.

"Wh-what is it?" Jemini shouted as I skidded into her and Max and knocked them both onto their backs.

"He's coming!" I shouted, trying to get my words to make more sense than the garbled, twisted way they came out. "The devil is coming!"

We all turned back toward the factory, and—sure enough—the devil and Needle-pinch were both floating eerily across the grasslands toward us.

"The forest!" Max screamed. "Let's run for the forest!"

"Why?"

"It beats staying here!"

"Good point!"

We fled for the edge of the trees, pausing briefly to wrench Max out of a narrow, muddy stream.

"Can the devil cross running water?" Jem-ini yelled as we ran on.

"Yeah," Max shouted back. "It's witches that can't."

"Great!"

We reached a thick clearing and all slid to a halt.

"Let's split up," I said determinedly. "You and Jemini go that way. I'll head east."

"Why?"

"Because the devil is after me, and I'd rather nobody else died on my account. Get it?"

"Got it."

"Good."

As Max and Jemini raced away, I bolted off through the trees, bellowing at the top of my voice, "Over here, you bearded, bony, jackal-toothed monkey-boy!"

My voice echoed through the trees but sounded weak even to me. I was seriously beginning to run out of decent insults.

The forest was lonely, dark, and deep, and I had some truly awesome hiding places to choose from.

So only the gods know why I selected a really obvious-looking bush right in the middle of the first tiny clearing I came across.

Thinking myself really clever for finding such an invisible position, I hunkered down and waited.

And waited.

And waited.

Eventually, after what felt like at least half an hour, I folded back some of the foliage and peered out into the clearing.

That was when a voice beside me said, "Who exactly are we looking for?"

I jumped out of my skin . . .

. . . and the bush.

REASON ... TO FIGHT FOR YOUR LIFE:

IT'S A PRETTY AMAZING GIFT

The devil strode around the clearing, clicking his fingers and humming quietly to himself.

As he did, the bush sprang up around me and curly tendrils of foliage snaked around my ankles and thighs, rooting me to the spot.

"I don't care what you do to me," I lied, my voice shaking pathetically in the shadowy clearing. "I'm just glad my friends got away from you."

The devil stopped in front of me and raised a bony finger to his lips.

"*Shhh*. Quiet down now, Ed. Your friends will be fine. My associate, Mr. Needlepinch, is kindly fetching them for me. I don't think they'll cause him too much trouble. He's a very . . . resourceful man."

I felt the tears rising inside me, a horrible sadness that I just wanted to fight and fight, but I knew I was too weak to go on.

"What do you want from me?" I said wretchedly. "I mean, I'm dead already."

The devil grinned. "Oh, but you could have been so much more, Ed. Just look at Kambo Cheapteeth. Now there was a dark warrior. And then there's you: pathetic, utterly pathetic. I gave you my own fingers and the opportunity to come over to my side and wreak havoc with them. You were only the second person to resist my will in the entire history of civilization. The first—"

"Was Evil Clive." As I finished the sentence, I just knew it was true. "Ha! You couldn't beat him, then! He resisted you as well! What did he have, two of your toes? Your manky elbow?"

The devil folded his arms and took a deep breath. Several curls of red smoke filtered down from his pointed nose.

"I'm going to inflict upon you the most savage and brutal punishment I can think of. And then I'm going to send you back to Mortlake."

I lowered my head and glared at him.

"There's nothing you can do to me which I haven't already—"

"Oh no, Ed, you're quite, quite wrong."

Max and Jemini appeared on the edge of the clearing. Both were walking in strange, guided steps and both had odd, faraway looks on their faces. Needlepinch fell into step behind them.

I swallowed, but my throat was dry.

"Please," I said, "I'll do anything, but please don't hurt my friends."

The devil chuckled.

"No harm will come to them, I can assure you," he said, a sick, disturbing smile on his face. "As much as I'd love to evict them both completely, there are rules—even for me."

Then he cracked his knuckles, took a deep breath, and pointed at Jemini.

A wall of flame shot from the end of his fingertips and completely engulfed her.

"Jemini!" I screamed. "No! JEMINIIIIII!"

The vampire-girl began to thrash around in a sudden explosion of panic, but the flames just became stronger, turned to a pale shade of orange, and intensified.

I closed my eyes and tried to block out the tortured cries of my doomed friend. When I opened them again, Jemini was gone.

I fell to my knees, a grim mixture of desperation, panic, and sadness driving me on.

"What have you done to her? What have you done?"

I scrambled to reach the patch of ground where Jemini had been standing, but the weeds and tendrils around the bush held me fast to the ground. I pressed myself away from the dirt and craned my neck until I could see Max's face.

"I'm so sorry, Max," I sobbed, trying to get the words through my choking throat. "I'm so sorry."

But Max simply wasn't there. He stared down at me with nothing more than a morbid, idle curiosity. His face was an empty shell.

The devil cackled wickedly and fired a second bolt of flame at Max.

This time I watched through tear-streaked eyes as my best friend in the world of the undead disappeared into fragments of floating air.

I laid on the dirty, mud-covered ground, awaiting whatever doom was about to be laid upon me. I didn't care anymore: my only friends were gone, and nothing else mattered.

I felt the devil's hand clasp my throat and lift me off the ground. I sagged, feeling my charred and devastated flesh hanging loosely on my rotted frame.

"Ed Bagley," said the devil, holding me aloft, his gleaming eyes piercing what was left of my immortal soul, "prepare to meet your fate."

A single tiny flame crept up the arm of the devil, but when it hit my flesh it exploded in a writhing, twisting, molten spew of furious fire.

The devil thrust me back onto my feet, and frantically I tore and scratched at my body, trying desperately to hammer out the pain . . . to no avail.

Piece by piece and chunk by terrifying chunk, my zombie flesh burned, melted, and ran away from me, leaving my ivory bones exposed to the moonlight.

A ghostly fire took everything that was left of the skin I'd squeezed pimples from, the skin I'd cut and grazed when I'd fallen from my bike, the skin I'd hugged in the cold and stretched in the sunlight . . .

. . . and all that was left were the bones beneath.

As I looked up at my tormentor, I was now nothing more than a human skeleton, a mirror image of Clive: grinning on the outside and sobbing on the inside at the cruelness of my inevitable fate.

But the worst was yet to come. . . .

The devil clapped his hands, dancing around the clearing with Needlepinch scampering along in his wake. Turning at the edge of the trees, he looked back and gave me a demonic wink.

"Goodbye, Ed Bagley," he said with a jovial nod. "I can't say you weren't fun to work with—but now, I'm afraid, is really not your time. Be grateful. Most people never get to experience this."

He pointed at me, and the searing, screaming bolt of fire that had taken Max and Jemini slammed into me, reducing my pitiful existence into memory and sorrow.

As the flames took the last of my vengeful spirit, I collapsed onto my bony knees. . . .

REASON...NOT TO QUESTION FATE:

IT MOVES IN MYSTERIOUS WAYS

The pain hit me.

A whirl of air slammed into me and I was flying through white light, screaming and thrusting every tiny pocket of strength I possessed into trying to fight the rushing onslaught that swept me back.

Two flashing blurs of energy spun past me, and suddenly, in a buzz of strange lightning, Max and Jemini were both just there, each of them holding on to me with arms outstretched, gritted teeth, and spit flying from their mouths.

"You're alive!" I shouted. "You're both alive!"

Max grinned, but his legs had begun to disintegrate behind him. It was like he was being dragged away, one molecule at a time.

"Ed! Hold on!"

I was overcome with a grim sense of despair. "I can't!" I yelled. "You two were the best friends I ever had. Do you hear me? Be nice to each other!"

Jemini screamed at me. "Just don't . . . let . . . go!"

Then she too began to dissolve, fragments of her spinning off into the blinding void.

"Jemini!" I shouted, wincing as Max's grip slipped from my other hand.

"Ed!"

"Max!"

Then, just like that, they were gone . . .

. . . and I cried out, collapsing onto asphalt with a yelping, curdled cry that made me sound like a five-year-old girl.

My leg was trapped.

I dropped the few school books that hadn't already fallen out of my arms and tried to twist my ankle out of the grate, but it was held firm between the bars.

That's when I heard the sound. A sound all too familiar—and getting louder by the second.

A truck. A very, very big truck heading along the road in my direction.

On an evening like tonight, in rain this torrential, the driver probably wouldn't even see me.

I renewed my efforts, scrambling around

like an idiot, frantically pulling at my leg until I felt the blood begin to flow from my ankle.

If I pulled any more, I'd probably lose my foot—and I really didn't want that to happen.

The truck was visible now, slamming along the road at a ridiculous speed.

I was doomed.

Mom always said those truckers were going to kill someone sooner or later—I just never thought it would be me.

"Stop!" I screamed, waving my arms back and forth like a lunatic. "Stop! Stop! STOPPPPPPPPPPPPPP!"

The rain hurtled down.

Thunder rumbled overhead.

I twisted and turned with my foot trapped firmly in the grate . . .

. . . and the truck rolled on.

I closed my eyes, screaming so much louder than I ever thought my voice could manage, waving my arms in vast, flapping circles while the end of my life raced toward me.

The truck slammed into me like a hundred-pound sledgehammer hitting a slice of bread . . .

. . . or it would have done—had the driver not swerved at the last moment and skidded to a noisy, hissing halt in the pouring rain.

My eyes remained tightly shut, my hands slowly dropping to my sides, as I realized two things very quickly.

First, that I wasn't nearly as scared as I probably should have been. And, second, that—amazingly—I was still alive.

The driver's side door of the truck swung open, and a pair of hefty leather boots hit the asphalt. The driver, a tall man in a long black overcoat, stomped across the road toward me.

"You insane, kid?" he spat. "I could've killed you!"

I looked up at the driver, allowing my shell-shocked expression and compromising position to speak for itself. "I didn't have much choice," I said, pointing to my leg.

The stranger nodded and moved around beside me. He reached down and pulled up the grate as if he was lifting a cup of coffee, then gently worked my ankle from between the bars until I'd managed to wriggle free. He even picked up my school books and shuffled them back into my arms.

"Thanks for that," I said, managing a weak smile. "Oh, and thanks for not killing me."

The stranger grinned.

"You should be more careful out here," he said, reaching into his overcoat and pulling out a battered-looking baseball cap which he thrust onto his head. "It's raining pretty hard, and if a truck like mine hits you, you're not exactly going to walk away."

He adjusted the cap until it was facing backward and gave me a wink. "Still, you know what they say. Whatever doesn't kill us makes us stronger. Take it easy." Then he turned and headed back to the truck.

"Is that your favorite band?" I called after him, pointing to the cap.

The stranger paused but didn't turn around.

"Dead Donkey?" he said. "Nah, not really. I just like their merchandise."

A few seconds later, the truck began to roll away toward the old factory.

"Weird guy," I muttered.

Then I bundled all the wet school books into my bag and headed for the distant lights of Mortlake.

As I walked along the same road where, just a few days earlier, I'd fought vampires and ghouls, I realized that something important had changed. It wasn't the half-familiar shape of the old town, the creepy way the trees all brushed together as if they were hugging for warmth, or even the pale wash of moonlight over the road. It wasn't the thunderous sound of the trucks starting up at the factory or the

y the wind and rain roared past at a luna-
: pace, obliterating practically all sight and
ound.

The thing that had changed was the little boy walking determinedly toward his old
home.

The thing that had changed was . . . me.

I didn't feel scared any more—not of other
kids, not of evil clowns, not even of the hor-
rors of Mortlake.

For some reason beyond my understand-
ing, the devil had given me a second chance.
Maybe he'd been impressed with my fighting
spirit or even the fact that I refused to aban-
don my friends. Maybe he just didn't like me
and wanted to keep me as far as possible from
the lands of the undead.

Whatever the reason, crazy, inept, clumsy
Ed Bagley had been given another shot at life.

And this time, I was determined to live it.